BOY,
MISSING

This World Book Day 2022 book
is a gift from your local bookseller and
Simon & Schuster Children's Books

Also by
Sophie McKenzie

Hide and Secrets
Truth or Dare

THE MISSING
SERIES

Girl, Missing
Sister, Missing
Missing Me

THE MEDUSA
PROJECT

The Set-Up
The Hostage
The Rescue
Hunted
Double-Cross
Hit Squad

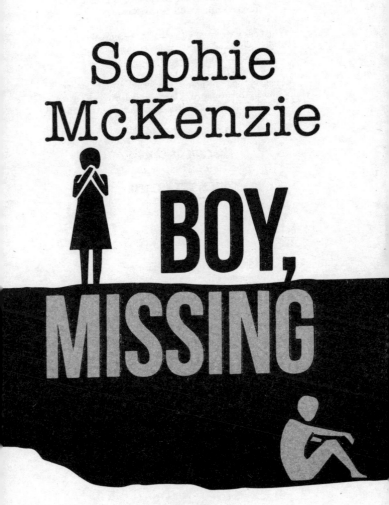

Sophie McKenzie

BOY, MISSING

SIMON &
SCHUSTER

First published in Great Britain in 2022 by Simon & Schuster UK Ltd
Text copyright © 2022 Sophie McKenzie

The right of Sophie McKenzie to be identified as the author
of this work has been asserted by her in accordance with sections
77 and 78 of the Copyright, Design and Patents Act, 1988.

1 3 5 7 9 10 8 6 4 2

Simon & Schuster UK Ltd
1st Floor, 222 Gray's Inn Road
London
WC1X 8HB

www.simonandschuster.co.uk
www.simonandschuster.com.au
www.simonandschuster.co.in

Simon & Schuster Australia, Sydney
Simon & Schuster India, New Delhi

A CIP catalogue record for this book
is available from the British Library.

PB ISBN 978-1-3985-0969-6

This book is a work of fiction. Names, characters, places
and incidents are either the product of the author's imagination
or are used fictitiously. Any resemblance to actual people
living or dead, events or locales is entirely coincidental.

Typeset in Goudy by M Rules
Printed and bound by CPI Group (UK) Ltd, Croydon, CR0 4YY

A NOTE FROM WORLD BOOK DAY

World Book Day's mission is to offer every child and young person the opportunity to read and love books by giving you the chance to have a book of your own.

To find out more, and get great recommendations on what to read next, visit **worldbookday.com**

World Book Day is a charity funded by publishers and booksellers in the UK and Ireland.

World Book Day is also made possible by generous sponsorship from National Book Tokens and support from authors and illustrators.

For Oscar and Matilda

ONE

I wedge myself into the tiny space between the empty gas cylinder and the back of our tent and pull Dad's waterproof jacket over me. It's a perfect hiding place: far enough away from the camp's central area to make my little cousin have to run around as he looks for me, but easy enough for him to find me once he's here.

'E-wen!' Charlie yells. 'I coming!' His three-year-old voice makes the *ls* in my name, Ellen, sound like *ws*. I can hear how excited he is. Hide-and-seek is his favourite game.

I huddle under the jacket and grin to myself. It's half-term, the last week in May, and I'm camping

1

in the countryside with my whole family. Not just Mum and Dad, but a bunch of aunts and uncles and cousins too. Their voices drift towards me: chattering and laughing as they make plans to go out for the day. After three days of rain, the sun has finally come out and everyone's in a good mood.

Well, almost everyone.

Through the mesh of Dad's jacket, I can just make out Charlie's yellow wellies, padding across the grass. I press myself against the tent fabric. Its sour smell mixes with the scent of damp earth. The yellow wellies draw closer. I hold my breath.

'I *finded* you!' Charlie squeals with delight. 'I *finded* you, E-wen!'

He tugs Dad's jacket off me and I make a face at him.

'You're too good at hide-and-seek,' I say. 'You're a *superstar* finder!'

'Superstar finder!' Charlie echoes. He hurls himself at me, all chubby arms and legs.

I hug him tight. His breath is hot on my ear. Charlie wriggles away and I ease myself out of my hiding place.

'Again! Again!' he cries.

'There you are, Charlie!' Auntie Mo appears around the tent. 'Now the sun's out, how would you like to go to the playground at Harmer, then get an ice cream?'

'Yay, ice cream!' Charlie cries. 'Go now, Mummy!'

Auntie Mo raises a weary eyebrow at me. 'I'm guessing that a trip to some swings with all the little ones isn't your idea of a perfect teenage afternoon, Ellie?'

I grin at her. Auntie Mo is my favourite aunt. She was there when I was born – and she's one of only two people who still call me Ellie. To everyone else now, I'm Ellen. My proper name.

'I already told Mum and Dad, I'll stay here,' I say. 'Mind the camp.'

'I totally get it,' Auntie Mo says with a sigh. 'I can't remember the last time I had a moment to myself. Talking of which, do you mind watching

Charlie for another few minutes? I just need to chuck a few things in a bag.'

'Sure,' I say.

Auntie Mo disappears.

''Nother hiding time!' Charlie demands.

'Okay, then, one last go. It's your turn to hide. I'll count.' I shoo him away. 'One ... Two ...'

Charlie speeds off as fast as his chunky little legs will carry him. As I carry on counting loudly, I watch him disappear around the corner of the tent. He's not the greatest at hide-and-seek, usually just picking a tent and snuggling under the nearest sleeping bag, making a Charlie-shaped bulge that isn't exactly hard to spot.

'Nine ... Ten,' I finish. 'Ready or not, here I come.'

I take a step towards the edge of the tent. A dark shadow blooms on the grass. As I look up, I get a split-second view of a black hoody hurtling towards me. Then *wham!* A bony shoulder rams against my side.

I stagger back, losing my balance. Gasping for breath, I fall to the ground.

TWO

I lie on the damp earth, winded. Two long, skinny legs in black jeans shuffle from side to side in front of me. I look up, into the scowling face of my cousin Harlan. A pair of huge headphones is jammed over his ears. He tugs them down and glares at me. A loud, messy guitar thumps a bassline into the air.

'You should look where you're going,' Harlan grunts.

Boomer, his black-and-white collie, bounds over and nudges at my arm. Boomer's barely more than a puppy and never stops moving.

'How about *you* look where *you're* going.'

I scramble to my feet, feeling my side. My bum is a little sore from where I landed, but otherwise I'm unhurt. Boomer licks at my hand.

'Sorry,' Harlan grunts. It's the most reluctant apology I've ever heard.

'Wow, thanks.' I make a face at him. 'I'm fine, by the way.'

Harlan frowns at the sarcasm in my voice. I raise my eyebrows. What is going on with him? He's been weird and bad-tempered ever since we arrived at the camp three days ago. Which makes no sense. Last week, we were still best friends. That's how it's always been – for thirteen years. Harlan and I were born within a few weeks and a few streets of each other. We're both only children and have, basically, grown up together. We even go to the same school. Shy, geeky Harlan has been my best friend since I can remember . . . right up until three days ago, when he arrived for our camping holiday acting like a different person.

'What were you doing?' he asks, still frowning.

'Playing hide-and-seek with Charlie,' I say,

patting Boomer's soft head. He nuzzles into my hand, then leaps from side to side, eager to play. At least the dog's pleased to see me. Unlike his owner.

'Oh.' The old Harlan would be asking to join in. The new version stares at me as if I'm mad. I gaze into his troubled eyes. Is that old Harlan even still in there?

'Would you like . . . ?' I begin, hopefully. 'Do you want to come and find Charlie with me?'

Harlan hesitates for a second, then sneers at me, lip curled in disgust. 'I'm not interested in doing anything with you.'

My jaw drops. Harlan turns and stomps away to his small, solo tent at the edge of the camp. I stare after him, a tornado of emotions tumbling inside me: I'm angry mostly, but underneath that I'm upset. It's like Harlan's taken our friendship and dumped it in a rubbish bin. It's hard to believe that less than a year ago, I was the very first person he came out to.

I suddenly remember Charlie and hurry around to the front of the tents, which are pitched in a rough circle around a central firepit. Most of the camp is here: Harlan's mum, Auntie Juniper, is chatting to my mum, while several of the other parents are busy stuffing hoodies and waterproofs into backpacks. Dad joins Mum and Juniper. He shows them something on his phone and the three of them laugh. Auntie Juniper wanders away and Dad slides his arm across Mum's shoulders. She leans her head towards his, winding her arm around his waist.

Where is *Charlie?* It's been a couple of minutes since I stopped counting down. I look inside the tent he shares with Auntie Mo. She's there, her back turned to me, rummaging in the pile of clothes in the corner. There's no sign of Charlie. I withdraw without speaking, then quickly look inside all the other tents.

He's not in any of them.

I stop outside Harlan's tent. The last thing I want is to talk to him again, but maybe Charlie snuck in here. I crouch down and peer between the canvas flaps. Harlan's lying on his back, eyes

8

closed, music leaking out of his headphones. Boomer is lying beside him, his eyes shut. Neither of them notice me looking in.

It's a tiny tent and Charlie definitely isn't inside.

Where is *he?* The field we're camping in is surrounded by open country, with a fenced-off copse of trees in the far corner. There's no way Charlie would be able to climb over the fence – and I'd surely be able to see him if he was in the next field.

'Okay, Charlie, you win!' I cry. 'Time to come out now.'

The only sound in response is the rustle of the trees in the breeze.

My chest tightens. I hurry around the whole outer perimeter of the camp, checking under every stray sleeping bag and behind both the storage areas. Still no sign of him. I head back to the central firepit, my heart hammering.

'Time to go!' Dad's cheery shout echoes through the mild, warm air.

Auntie Mo emerges from her tent, a hefty

backpack over her shoulder. She smiles at me. 'Can you get Charlie, please? He's going to love the playground.'

I stare at her. 'He's still hiding,' I say, anxiety spiralling up to my throat. 'I'll find him.'

Auntie Mo nods, distractedly. 'Thanks, Ellie.' She frowns. 'Oh, his jacket.' She dives back inside her tent.

I hurry through the camp again as everyone strolls to their cars. Charlie *must* be here somewhere. I pass Harlan's tent again. This is all his fault for getting in my way and delaying me.

And then I spot it: a stray yellow welly on the grass near the cars.

I stare at the boot, numb with terror.

'Ellie?' It's Auntie Mo.

I look up. She's smiling at me, eyebrows raised expectantly. And I can't bear to speak, to watch the smile fall from her face and the fear fill her eyes. But what choice do I have?

'Ellie?' she asks again, her voice faltering.

'It's Charlie,' I say. 'He's gone!'

THREE

'Charlie! Charlie!' My voice disappears into a gust of wind.

'Charlie!' Auntie Mo is calling too, panic in her voice.

Guilt seizes me like a fist. 'Charlie?' I shriek. 'Where are you?'

Everyone stares at me. Most of my aunts and uncles just look confused, but Mum clutches her forehead, her eyes filling with the same terror that's all over Auntie Mo's face. And then, rising into the air, comes Dad's deep yell:

'Charlie's here! Under Rory's car.'

Auntie Mo and I break into a run. The sleek,

shiny Audi that belongs to Uncle Rory is parked at the end of the cars – all of which are older and more battered-looking. As I race up, Charlie is scrambling out from under the vehicle, helped by Dad. Charlie jumps up, grinning from ear to ear.

'I did it!' he cries. 'Superstar hiding!'

Relief floods through me, draining away the panic and leaving my legs suddenly wobbly.

Auntie Mo rushes forward and grabs Charlie by the arm.

'What were you *thinking*?' she demands, her voice breaking. 'You know you're not allowed anywhere near the cars.'

Charlie's triumphant expression slides into a sulky frown. He glances up, sees everyone looking at him, and kicks at the ground. 'Superstar hiding,' he mutters.

'It was my fault,' I say quickly. 'I should have reminded Charlie he was only supposed to hide in the camp.'

'I hope he didn't scratch the car.' That's Helena, Uncle Rory's annoying girlfriend. She's all flouncy hair and designer jacket and has been looking down her nose at everyone since she and my uncle arrived this morning.

'He's only a toddler,' Dad points out.

'We should get going if we're going to make lunch,' Helena says.

'Of course,' Uncle Rory says, gazing at her adoringly.

Mum shakes her head. She has no more time for her brother's latest girlfriend than the rest of us.

'Let's fetch your wellies, then get you inside the car, shall we?' Auntie Mo tugs Charlie away.

'Okay, everyone ready to go?' Dad asks.

The group dissolves as the other families melt away, fetching last-minute items from their tents or wrangling small kids into the backs of cars. Rory and Helena drive off first. They've planned lunch at a posh restaurant thirty miles away, while everyone else is at the playground.

As my aunts and uncles and cousins make their way to the cars, I'm left with just Mum and Dad. After the earlier turmoil, I'm calming down. In a minute, all the adults will be gone and I'll have the whole afternoon to myself. Well – myself and grumpy Harlan. Mum and Dad pick up their bags and look at each other.

'That was scary there for a moment, Jam,' Mum says with a relieved smile.

'Yeah.' Dad grins. 'For a second, I thought Rory's girlfriend was going to come with us.'

Mum laughs. Now I'm older, I've started to notice these private moments where they share a look or a joke with each other. They've been together since they were my age and they're still all loved up.

Sometimes it's nice. Mostly it's embarrassing.

'Are you sure you don't want to come with us, Ellen?' Mum asks.

I nod.

Dad frowns. 'Really? It feels wrong leaving you.'

'I'll be fine,' I insist. 'Anyway you've already got Charlie and Auntie Mo. There'll be more room in the car without me.'

'Okay,' Mum says, 'if you're sure.'

'Keep your phone switched on,' Dad urges.

'Is it charged?' Mum asks. 'I left one of the portable chargers on your sleeping bag, and we're going to find somewhere to top up the other one.'

'It's charged,' I say, rolling my eyes, though in fact I haven't checked the bars since I got up.

Mum nods, then gives me a hug. 'Okay, sweetie, see you later.' She turns to Dad. 'I'm just going to the loo.' She hurries across the field. Dad clears his throat.

'Couple of things, Ellen,' he says. 'Firstly, phone on.'

'You already said that.'

'Secondly, it's fine to take a stroll across the fields nearby, but don't be tempted to climb over the barrier and go into those woods.' Dad gestures to the fenced-off copse of trees at the far corner of the field. 'They open out straight on to an old limestone quarry with a hundred-metre drop. The farmer we're renting from says it's very dangerous.'

'I *know*,' I grumble. 'You've told me a million times already.'

'Okay.' Dad nods. 'And thirdly, it would be really helpful if while we're away you could deal with the rubbish that's built up around the camp.' He smiles at me hopefully. 'I'm sure Harlan will help. The two of you can get it done in no time, if you work together.'

Work together with Harlan? *No way*. Surely Dad must have noticed how weird Harlan's being with me.

'Are you serious?'

'Absolutely.' Dad frowns. 'What's the problem?'

I stare at him, horrified. '*Everything*.'

FOUR

Dad looks at me, clearly shocked. 'I don't understand, Ellen. You and Harlan are best friends.'

How can he not have noticed how Harlan's been behaving since we got here?

'We're not friends any more,' I snap. 'You wouldn't believe how he acted earlier. We crashed into each other. Like *literally*. And Harlan didn't even apologize properly.'

'Well, that doesn't sound like something worth falling out over.' Dad sighs.

'It's *more* than that,' I insist. 'It's as if he's mad at me for no reason. He's been like it since we arrived.'

'Well, *something* must have happened,' Dad persists.

I frown, thinking back to the last time I saw Harlan before we came on the camping holiday. It was in the cafeteria at school on Wednesday, during lunch break. He wasn't acting weird then, though I don't remember seeing him much for the rest of the week. Which, now I come to think of it, is strange in itself. Normally we speak every day.

'Did you argue about anything recently?' Dad asks.

'No.' I try to remember what Harlan and I talked about that day. Something about homework, I think; and a song we'd just heard; and a boy, Jake, in my form, who Harlan said was very cute. 'We definitely didn't have a fight about anything,' I say sullenly, 'but even if we had, it wouldn't excuse Harlan being so mean.'

'Well, perhaps doing something together will give you a chance to sort things out,' Dad says, wearily. 'I'd like you to clear out the firepit; then take all the ash, plus the food waste and recycling to the big bins. The farmer we're renting off asked if we'd keep on top of our litter.'

'But that's all the way over by the farmhouse,' I moan, staring across the field to the squat, stone Mild Meadow Farm. It's the only building for miles. 'It'll take *ages*.'

'Not if you and Harlan work together.'

'Didn't you hear what I said?' I snap. 'Harlan's being horrible.'

'Then sharing a job gives you an opportunity to find out what's wrong.' Dad gives me a stern look. 'I'm not arguing with you, Ellen. The rubbish needs taking across the field, and it sounds to me like you need to ask Harlan what's wrong and *listen* to what he says.' He smiles. 'You remind me of your mum when she was your age: always sure she had the answers to everything.'

'I'm not like that,' I say.

Dad raises his eyebrows, clearly unconvinced. 'Sometimes, Ellen, you have to be patient and let people work things out for themselves.' He pauses. 'And did I mention *listening*?'

I'm about to protest again, but I can see in Dad's eyes there's no point arguing. I turn away, feeling mutinous.

All the vehicles except ours have now driven off. Across the field, Mum appears. 'Bye, Ellen!' she calls out, heading straight for our car, where Auntie Mo and Charlie are already waiting.

'Right, we'll be going. Bye, sweetheart.' Dad gives me a quick hug and turns away.

I stomp back to the tents, as the sound of our car driving away fills the air.

I'd been so looking forward to having the afternoon to myself, and now I'm going to have to spend ages on Dad's irritating tasks. Unless I do what he suggested and ask Harlan to help – the idea of which makes my skin crawl.

Dad has no idea.

No way am I asking Harlan for any assistance. I'll just get things done as fast as possible, starting with the firepit. I grab a brush.

After a few minutes, all the ash is swept up and in a bag. I haul it over to the food-waste area at the end of the camp. Three large sacks are already full and sealed, with another just started. How can such a small group of people create so much rubbish in just a few days?

I glance over at Harlan's tent. The annoying hiss of his music floats towards me. Muttering under my breath, I pick up one of the sealed sacks. I can just about carry it, but there's no way I can manage either of the others – or the bag full of ash – as well. Which means four separate trips. Gritting my teeth with the effort, I start dragging the first sack across the field. Boomer appears, gambolling along beside me for a moment, then darting away to explore a scent. As I heave the bag up, over the gate, the bottom rips. A trickle of disgusting brownish liquid seeps on to my trainers.

Great.

I groan out loud. Across the field, Boomer lifts his head, then lowers it again, more interested in the patch of hedge he's sniffing than my misery.

Surely this day can't get any worse?

FIVE

I stand in the field. The air is warm, but dark clouds are scudding across the sky, so it's probably going to rain again later. Most likely just about the time I finish my jobs for Dad, which means I'll end up stuck inside a tent for the rest of the afternoon.

It's not fair.

Anger burns in my chest. There's no reason why Harlan shouldn't carry at least *one* of these heavy sacks. After all, he was supposed to help. I turn on my heel. I march over to Harlan's tent – Boomer lolloping at my side – and yank back the opening.

Harlan is still lying on his back, eyes shut and

headphones over his ears. He must sense the change of light because his eyes open. He sees me and sits up, tugging his headphones down. 'What d'you want, Ellen?' he grunts.

His words feel like a knife. Along with Auntie Mo, Harlan's the only person I still let call me by my old pet name, Ellie. And now, out of the blue, he's stopped using it.

Boomer bounds past me and hurls himself at Harlan as if he hasn't seen him for a week. Harlan ruffles his ears, absently, still gazing up at me. I glare back at him.

'My dad said we have to take the ash from the firepit and the food waste to the farm bins. And I've already swept the ash and tried to take one bag of rubbish, which split all over me, so you need to at least do *some* of the work.'

Harlan's expression grows more sullen. 'Uncle Jam didn't say anything to me.'

'Well, you were in here sulking when we were talking,' I point out. 'If you'd been outside with everyone else, you'd have heard him.'

Harlan says nothing, but the contempt in his eyes is obvious. Something twists in my stomach. I love school now, but I don't know if I'd have survived my first week in Year Seven without Harlan by my side. We've always told each other everything: our worries, our hopes, our crushes. But now he clearly can't stand the sight of me, and the worst thing is, I have no idea why.

'Have I done something to upset you?' I ask.

A look of surprise fills Harlan's eyes, then the scorn floods back. 'Like you don't know what you did,' he snarls.

'I *don't* know.' The pain I felt a few seconds ago morphs into intense frustration. 'Tell me, please.'

There's a brief pause. A seagull squawks overhead and a gust of wind flaps at the tent. The sun beats down on the back of my neck.

'Harlan?' I ask again, my voice breaking. '*Please* talk to me.'

Harlan meets my gaze for a final moment, then looks away. 'You told Jake in your form room that I fancy him,' he mutters.

'No, well ...' I hesitate. Now I'm thinking about it, I *did* chat to Jake at some point during our Maths class, soon after Harlan confided his feelings at lunch break last Wednesday. 'I just told him how great you are.'

'It was more than that.'

I frown, trying to remember. 'I said you were an amazing person, and Jake asked if you were with anyone, which I thought meant he liked you, so I may have mentioned that you'd told me you thought he was fit, but—'

'But *nothing*. You thought that just cos there's one other person in our year who's out, we should obviously hook up, so you stuck your nose in like you always do.'

'That's not fair,' I protest. 'I only thought ... think ... that you'd make a great couple. Jake's good-looking and ... and really nice. I was just trying to help.'

'Of *course* you were!' Harlan snarls sarcastically. 'Because you always think you know what's best for everyone. You're so *self-involved*.'

My stomach falls away as I stare at him, tears pricking my eyes.

'How can you think that?' I demand. 'What is *wrong* with you? I thought the reason you've been behaving like a total jerk since you got here was something *serious*, but this … You're completely overreacting. I was trying to do something nice for you and now you're being ridiculous and mean and … and … it's *pathetic*.'

Harlan looks at me again, his eyes narrowing. 'You're the one who's pathetic.' He scrambles to his feet, grabbing his sunglasses with one hand and his phone with the other. He hurls himself to the tent entrance, pushing past me as he clambers out, then storms away.

'Where are you going?' I shout after him.

'Leave me alone,' Harlan yells over his shoulder. He strides angrily across the field, his shoulders hunched. Boomer scampers after him.

I watch them leave, rage roiling up through my chest, into my throat, choking me.

'I hate you!' I yell. 'I hate you!'

Harlan doesn't look round. He's heading for the fenced-off copse of trees that Dad has been warning us all week not to go into.

I turn away, my breath coming in huge, furious heaves. The sun is fierce on my face as I survey the camp. I had been so looking forward to being here for a few hours on my own. But now I have to take all the bags of stinking waste to the farm bins by myself. On top of which, Harlan has made it clear that our friendship is totally cancelled.

SIX

As I return to the camp after lugging the final bag to the farm bins, a few drops of rain spatter on to my head. Stupid Harlan and his stupid dog aren't back. They must still be in the forbidden wood. I growl under my breath. *I don't care what Harlan does.* I splash some water on a cloth and wipe at the mess on my shoe, but the stain doesn't budge.

As I chuck down the cloth, my phone pings. A text from Dad:

You and Harlan doing okay? Love you x

I ignore the message. If Dad hadn't forced me to do his stupid jobs, I wouldn't have had that row with Harlan.

> Auntie J has been calling Harlan. Can you get him to ring her? ☀ Gorgeous day here in Harmer. We'll probably stay an extra hour then shop for food on way home. You guys all right?

He's sent two now, so grudgingly I reply:

> Fine, see you later.

At least the delay in their return means I've got some me-time back. I wander around the camp. What shall I do now? I attempt to check my social media, but the internet connection is so slow it's impossible. Frustrated, I ransack Mum's stash of sweet treats, but all I find is a pack of croissants, which are two days past their sell-by date and dry as paper. Irritated, I try playing music loudly on

Dad's portable speakers, but the wind whisks the sound away.

Truth is, it's boring here, all by myself. At least the rain has stopped. For now. I wander towards the fenced-off wood. Harlan and Boomer have been gone almost an hour.

What are they doing in there?

I stand in front of the fence. If there's one thing that would annoy Harlan, it'd be me distracting his dog from whatever stupid game they're playing.

'Boomer!' I yell, then wait for an answering 'woof' and the sight of his familiar furry face emerging from the trees.

But Boomer doesn't appear.

The parting words I shouted at Harlan circle my head: *I hate you.*

Yes, Harlan was mean, but my words were mean too. Guilt pricks at my conscience. I examine the padlocked gate in the middle of the fence. A big DANGER – KEEP OUT sign is nailed to the top.

The sun is going in and out fast now: one minute

winking brightly on the leaves; the next vanishing behind another cloud. As it emerges once more, something on the ground just ahead of me glints. I hurry over. Harlan's sunglasses are lying on the ground, beside a freshly dug hole under the fence. Did Boomer dig that? I'm pretty certain Harlan didn't have him on a lead when he stormed out of the camp. I bet Boomer got a sniff of an interesting scent on the other side of the fence and clawed his way underneath. Harlan must have dropped his sunnies hurrying after him. Strange he didn't pick them up, though.

'Boomer!' I place the sunglasses carefully into my shirt pocket. 'Harlan! Boomer!'

Nothing, not even the sound of a distant bark. I glance across to the DANGER – KEEP OUT sign. Dad said something about a steep drop into an old limestone quarry. There's no way Harlan would go anywhere near that – he's terrified of heights.

Should I call Dad? It would totally serve Harlan right if I snitched on him. Except that if I call my parents and tell them Harlan's inside the forbidden

SEVEN

The call goes to voicemail. I lean over the fence. 'Harlan?' I call. '*Harlan*, come here. This isn't funny!'

Still no reply.

'Boomer!' I yell, at the top of my voice.

Nothing.

This is really weird. Apart from anything else, there's no way Harlan would be able to keep the dog quiet. Overhead, the sun disappears behind a large cloud. I squint into the dim light of the trees. Surely if I'm careful, I'll be able to avoid the sheer drop Dad warned us about.

I clamber over the fence. Under the trees the air

is cooler and smells of damp earth. I walk slowly, twigs crunching under my feet, letting my eyes get used to the gloom. A breeze rustles the leaves above my head. Hardly any sky is visible through the branches. I call Harlan's phone again.

The answering ring is close. I hurry to the sound echoing spookily through the air. I've walked barely five minutes from our family camp, but it suddenly feels like I'm in the middle of nowhere. The trees are thinning out. Through the gaps I spot the quarry and gasp. It's huge – an ugly, grey, hollowed-out stretch of land with breathtakingly steep sides.

Harlan's phone is right on the edge. I hang up and walk over. The barren hillside falls sharply away beneath me. My stomach lurches. There's no way Harlan would have voluntarily come this close to such a severe drop. I pick it up and look at the home screen. It's flashing up all my missed calls – and Auntie Juniper's.

My heart lodges in my throat. Harlan might ditch his sunglasses to save Boomer, but I've *never* seen him without his phone.

I stand in the cool of the trees. Something is very wrong.

'Harlan! Boomer!' My voice is whipped away by the wind.

Nothing.

The grey stone quarry is completely deserted. I lean carefully out from between the trees and stare down the rocky incline. The sight of the massive drop sends goosebumps racing up my arms. I grab the nearest tree. No wonder the wood is fenced off.

A tree with half its roots exposed lies a few metres to the left. The ground that once buried them must have slid down into the chasm below. Gripping my tree trunk, I peek over the edge. Yes, the whole slope of the quarry there is covered in mud, all the way down to the bottom.

I shiver. Did Harlan and his dog fall down this steep hill?

My palms are sweaty against the rough bark of the tree.

'Harlan! Boomer!'

I listen, ears straining. A faint sound drifts towards me.

Is that a human cry?

I can't tell. It could easily have been a bird.

A metre or so to my left, the slope is gentler. I shove Harlan's phone deep into my trouser pocket and step carefully in that direction. *Maybe I'll—*

Without warning, the soft, damp earth crumbles under my feet.

I'm sliding. Fast. Rocky ground bumping underneath me. Bruising my legs and my side. Faster. I flail out with my arms, but it's impossible to grab a hold. Stones scrape like knives at my bare arms as I hurtle down the incline.

There's nothing I can do to stop my fall.

EIGHT

*T*hump. I land on my side in a dirty puddle at the bottom of the quarry. Winded, I lie in the squelchy earth, trying to catch my breath, then struggle on to my elbows. I pat myself down. I feel bruised all over, but – amazingly – I'm not seriously hurt. The phones – mine and Harlan's – are also undamaged, though Harlan's sunglasses are cracked in two.

The quarry rises around me on all sides. Even the banks that aren't insanely steep are crazily high. My heart thuds hard.

How on earth am I going to get back up to the wood and the campsite?

I push the thought out of my head. I'll face that challenge when I have to. First, I need to find Harlan.

Scrambling to my feet, I wipe my hands on my muddy trousers. I'm shivering, though whether that's from the shock of my fall or because the air is cooling, I'm not sure. High above me, dark clouds are now filling the sky. I stamp my feet and hug my arms around my chest, then take a couple of deep breaths.

Dad taught me to do that. He says it's the best thing when you need to calm down: to feel your feet planted on the ground and let the air flow in and out of your lungs.

It works. Kind of. At least I stop shivering. I take another look around. The ground to my right is spattered with mud that must have slid down from the top of the quarry. About four metres above it is a broad, thin, rocky overhang, covered with thick clods of damp earth. If I'd fallen there, I'd have flown off the overhang and plummeted to the ground beneath.

I shiver again. You could easily break your arm falling like that.

Or your neck.

I gulp. 'Harlan! Boomer!'

My voice echoes, bouncing off the steep hill behind me.

'Hey!' A faint but familiar cry drifts towards me from the dirt-strewn area beneath the muddy overhang.

'Harlan!' A swell of relief rises inside me, choking my chest and throat. I hurry towards the sound of his voice. 'Are you okay?'

'Fine,' he calls back. 'Come here – I need your help!'

I peer into the shadowy area under the rock, a shiver shuddering through me. I've always hated dark, enclosed spaces, ever since I was little and accidentally locked myself into our understairs cupboard. 'Where are you? Where's Boomer?'

'In the cave. *Come on!*'

'What cave?' I yell.

'The entrance is right in front of you!' Harlan

shouts. There's an impatience in his voice. 'Get in here!'

Charming. No way am I going to let him get all snarky with me when I nearly died trying to find him. I squint into the darkness under the overhang. Harlan's right. There's a tiny gap in the rock face – a little taller and wider than I am. It forms an arch-like entrance into what must be Harlan's cave.

'Hello!' I call through the passageway. My voice echoes back at me. *Hel-lo-lo-lo . . .*

'Hurry up!' Harlan's reply is loud and clear.

And more than a little irritating.

I take a step inside. The air here is damp and still, the roof of the cave only just above my head. 'I can't see anything!'

'Walk towards this!' A tiny prick of light flickers ahead.

Slowly and carefully, I feel my way along the passage, my eyes fixed on the glow.

'Come *on!*' Harlan calls.

Part of me wants to yell back something

sarcastic, but I keep my focus on getting through the passage. One step. Then another. Ahead of me, I hear Boomer's muffled bark.

Without warning, the light ahead goes out.

'Hey!' I yell, panic soaring into my voice.

'Okay, okay, hang on!' Another light sparks. This time I hear the strike and flare of a match.

'Yeah, I see.' I speed up and the passageway opens into a large cave. I spot Harlan at last. He's crouched down, the match in his hand casting shadows over his face. He smiles with relief as he sees me and, for a second, it's as if all the tensions of the past few days fall away and we're back, the best of friends, like we used to be.

'Thank goodness,' I say. 'I was so worr—' I stop with a yelp as the match burns through and we're plunged into darkness. 'Light another!'

'I'm almost out. Don't you have your phone?' Harlan sounds impatient again.

'Right.' Of course, why didn't I think of that myself? I fish my mobile out of my pocket and fumble for the torch.

Light fills the space. I swing the torch round. The cave is bigger than I was expecting. Its uneven limestone walls glisten damply, a yellowy-grey colour. Harlan is crouched down beside a large rock at the back of the cave. He holds up his hand to shield his face from the glare of my torch. I lower the light and catch sight of Boomer's tail thumping against the ground at Harlan's feet.

I shine my torch up at his hind legs. His haunches – and the rest of his big, furry frame – are hidden behind the large rock.

'Are you really okay?' I ask, hurrying over. 'Is Boomer all right?'

'He's stuck,' Harlan says.

Boomer gives a woof, presumably on hearing me say his name, but it's not his normal enthusiastic barking.

'Is he hurt?' Boomer gazes mournfully up at me. *Poor thing* – his front paw is wedged between the back wall of the cave and the rock.

'I don't know.' Harlan sounds anxious.

I reach down and stroke Boomer's soft head. He lets out a low whimper. I lower my hand to his paw, but I can't move it.

Harlan's right. The dog is totally trapped.

NINE

'Give me that light, will you?' Harlan asks. 'I'm out of matches and I lost my phone earlier.'

'Yeah, I found it at the top of the quarry,' I say, tugging the mobile out of my pocket.

Harlan takes it with a grunt, frowning as he swipes to the torch app.

'What happened?' I ask. 'I saw the hole Boomer dug under the fence, but—'

'I chased him through the trees,' Harlan explains, shining the light from his mobile on to Boomer's paw. 'He was playing – loving it, the idiot – until the ground at the top of the quarry gave way and he fell. So I rushed over and when I saw how steep it was I got …' He stops.

'Frightened? Dizzy?' I ask, remembering his fear of heights. 'Is that why you fell too?'

Harlan shrugs, saying nothing. His face is sullen in the dim light. My heart sinks. A week ago, he'd have had no problem admitting his vulnerabilities to me.

Harlan leans down, frowning as he tries to ease Boomer's paw out from between the cave wall and the large rock. Boomer scrabbles back with his hind legs, but it's no use.

'He's completely stuck,' I say.

Harlan glances up at me, his scowling face wreathed in shadows. 'No kidding, genius.'

Ignoring this, I say, 'I was leaning out over the quarry, trying to see where you were. I fell too.'

Harlan takes no notice. He sits back on his heels 'When I picked myself up, Boomer had already sniffed out this cave and got stuck. Stupid dog.' He pats Boomer's fur, then looks up at me, grimacing. 'That's why I didn't come out when I heard you calling. I didn't want to leave him.'

He turns back to the dog.

'Right,' I say slowly, 'so you just left me on my own to risk my neck.'

Harlan frowns. 'Well, that's typical,' he mutters.

'What do you mean?' Irritation rises inside me. The least Harlan could do is appreciate my trying to find him.

'I mean,' Harlan says scornfully, 'that everything isn't all about *you*, Ellen.'

'I'm not making *anything* about me. I'm just pointing out that if you'd come outside and shouted up to me earlier, I could have brought something that might help Boomer, instead of nearly dying by falling down the quarry.'

Harlan falls silent for a moment. Boomer wriggles and whimpers again. Harlan's free hand rubs his back in long, slow, soothing strokes. I sink my own hand into the dog's deep fur, feeling the warmth of his neck. I pat the top of his head, and Boomer snuffles, turning into my hand.

'What would you have brought,' Harlan asks at last, 'that would have helped get Boomer free?'

I jump up, infuriated. 'I don't know. What do we need?'

'I don't know.' Harlan shrugs. 'Not that it matters, seeing as we don't have anything anyway. And before you ask, the rock's too heavy to move. I've tried.'

'Maybe if we try to move it together?' I suggest.

Harlan looks sceptical, but nods.

'Come on.' I place my mobile against the back wall of the cave, tilting it so the light from the torch app shines as widely as possible.

The two of us stand side by side, squaring up to the rock. Harlan puts his palms on the top and I position myself beside him, my hands gripping the cold limestone. Boomer gazes up at us, his eyes scared but trusting.

'We're going to get you out, Boomer,' I reassure him, though deep down I don't feel anywhere near so confident.

'On three,' I say. Harlan braces himself. I grip the rock harder. 'One. Two. *Pull!*'

TEN

I tug at the rock, my knuckles white in the soft glow of our phones. It doesn't budge.

Harlan curses, his voice full of despair.

Boomer whimpers, trying to scrabble away. His paw is still stuck.

'Keep trying,' I pant, pulling harder at the rock.

'I am!' Harlan snaps. He moves so that more of his body is behind the rock, the light from his mobile flaring across the cave.

I grit my teeth. *What an idiot!* Still, I want to help poor Boomer get free, so I take a deep breath and shift sideways so that my whole arm is over the rock.

'Again!' I call out. 'One. Two. Go!'

With a grunt, I give it everything I've got. The limestone digs into my hands. Pain sears through me. The rock scrapes a fraction across the stone floor.

'Almost!' Harlan's voice rises with excitement.

Another heave. *There.* With a yelp, Boomer wriggles backwards, his paw freed. He rises on to all fours, turning this way and that as if checking he's really free.

'Hey, boy!' Harlan calls him and the dog trots obediently over. Harlan falls to his knees and rubs his hands across the top of Boomer's head. The dog whines up at him, licking his hands.

I rub my sore palms and look properly at Harlan. He's as filthy as I am – with grubby smears down his cheeks and arms, but his eyes shine in the dim light of the torch app. I have a sudden, sharp memory of us playing together when Boomer was a puppy: Harlan grinning with delight, his big, brown eyes full of fun as we raced around the park for what felt like hours. He was always shyer and less sporty than me – when we were little, I made sure he didn't get left out at parties, or in games. But he was also better at lots of stuff too, like reading. And homework. And understanding complicated science data. For as long as I can remember, he's been by my side, through everything.

Surely a friendship that strong can't be destroyed by one, tiny, well-meant act?

Surely, even if Harlan thinks I was wrong to talk to Jake, he isn't right to get so angry about it?

Surely, now I've helped rescue Boomer, we'll be okay again?

'D'you think Boomer's all right?' I drop down to the ground, taking the dog's front leg in my hands and examining the paw that was trapped.

'I think he's fine,' Harlan says. 'Let him go and we'll see.'

We take our hands off the dog, who immediately trots around the cave, sniffing at the ground.

'Look! No limping,' Harlan says with a grin.

I smile back at him. 'We did it,' I say.

The grin vanishes from Harlan's face. He turns

to me. 'Yeah, you totally saved the day, Ellen,' he says, his voice suddenly fierce. 'I just looked after him for like, an hour, before you turned up. But no ... you're right – we did it.'

My jaw drops. 'Why are you being so mean?' I demand. 'You know I wasn't saying that I did everything. I just meant that we got Boomer out of being trapped ...' I pause. 'Are you seriously being like this just because of Jake? I already explained that I only talked to him because I was trying to help you.'

Harlan ignores me, padding over to Boomer again and stroking his back.

'Let's get out of here,' he says.

Hurt, I walk over to where my phone is still propped up next to the rock we shifted. No signal.

'You should call your mum when we get outside,' I say, picking it up. 'There were loads of missed calls from her on your mobile.'

'Wow, thanks,' Harlan says, snarkily. 'I'd never have worked that out for myself.'

Tears prick at my eyes. Tears that I don't want

Harlan to see. I turn slowly, letting the light from my mobile dance over the walls of the cave. The colours are amazing: gold and ivory and steel-grey, all blended together. Thunder rumbles outside, then creates a crack so loud it makes me start. Boomer lets out a whimper. Seconds later the sound of pounding rain outside echoes around the cave.

Harlan makes a face. 'Great,' he grumbles.

I sigh. 'Rain's going to make that quarry harder to climb, even where the slope isn't so steep.'

Harlan gives a curt nod. 'Come on, then. The sooner we—'

Another clap of thunder, louder than the last, makes us jump. Boomer lets out a frantic volley of barks. He disappears through the passageway, racing towards the exit. Harlan and I follow. As Boomer bounds outside and out of sight, strange sounds echo around us: cracking and shifting and sliding sounds.

I look up at the rough stone ceiling above our heads. 'What's that noise?'

'Dunno.' Harlan frowns. 'It doesn't sound good though. We should—' He stops abruptly as the low roof of the passageway seems to shake. I stare at the gap Boomer has just scampered through. I gasp. Lumps of mud are piling up outside the exit. Blocking our way out.

'What's happening?' My voice rises in panic.

'I think it's a landslide.' The fear in Harlan's voice mirrors my own. 'The rain must be driving the mud off the top of the overhang.'

We look at each other.

'Run!' I yell.

ELEVEN

We race along the passageway to the exit. Huge splats of earth are mounting up outside.

'*Faster!*' Harlan shouts.

The end of the word is drowned out as a large chunk of limestone falls on to the ground just outside the exit. A second later, another thuds on top of it. More rocks cascade down outside, plunging the passage into darkness. The only light bounces from my phone, spiking weird shapes all around us.

Harlan skids to a halt, grabbing my arm. His eyes are wide with terror.

'Let me go!' Panic swirls inside me. 'We have to get out!'

'It's too late.' Harlan drags me back towards the cave. A terrible heaving sound echoes around us. Bigger stones fall, great slabs of limestone thudding down all around us. Fear clutches at my throat.

'We can get out!' I push past him. 'Come on!'

'No!' Harlan yells. 'It's too dangerous.'

'But we'll be *trapped* in here! We have to try.'

'If we try, we'll be *killed* by one of those falling rocks.'

My heart gallops in my chest. I shine the torch app across the mud-and-stone barrier between us and the quarry. There are no gaps, no way of crawling through.

No way out.

The hairs on the back of my neck prickle.

'Are you okay?' The fear in Harlan's voice sends a wave of panic spiralling up my body. Taking a long, shaky breath, I force myself to face him. His eyes are dark, his face ghostly in the torchlight.

'I'm fine,' I say. 'What about Boomer, though – do you think he got out all right?'

Harlan meets my gaze, anxiety filling his eyes. 'I hope so.' He pauses. 'What are we going to do?'

I draw myself up. My whole body is trembling, but I can't let myself fall apart. I look at my phone. There's no signal in here. No way to call for help.

'Let's see if there's another way out.'

I don't speak the thought in my head: *If there isn't, then we're dead.*

'Okay.' Harlan nods. He takes his phone out and switches on his torch app too. 'Let's go slowly round the cave,' he suggests. He points to the left. 'I'll go this way – you go the other.'

The lights flicker as we walk the perimeter of the large, gloomy space.

'My battery's almost gone,' Harlan says with a groan. 'How's yours?'

'About forty per cent.' I grimace to myself. I should have checked when Mum asked me to earlier. Charged it properly. I stare at the stone wall ahead of me. There's not so much as a chink of a gap. 'Can you see any openings?'

'No,' Harlan says. 'Wait. What's this?'

I hurry over to the fold in the rock where he's standing. There's a low opening, hip-height and just wide enough to crawl through. I crouch down and stare into the narrow space. It's impossible to see more than a metre or so ahead – terrifying. I take a deep breath and stand back up.

'Where do you think it leads?'

'Outside, hopefully.' Harlan pauses, then says shakily, 'Anyway, it's our only chance.'

'Right.'

'We should turn off one of our phones,' Harlan suggests. 'Conserve the batteries as long as possible.'

'Turn yours off,' I say quickly. I can't bear the thought of not having a light with me.

Harlan does as I suggest. 'Ready?'

I grit my teeth. 'Let's go.'

TWELVE

I drop down to all fours and crawl into the tunnel. The damp stone is cold under my knees. My phone is between my teeth, the torch app casting a spooky flicker of light along the ground ahead. I shuffle a few inches, but the walls are so close. *Too* close. Like they're pressing in on me. Fear surges up from my belly, sending a tornado of panic down my arms and legs, and up into my head. I stop moving. My breath is coming in jagged pants and gasps.

Behind me Harlan calls, 'What's up? You okay?'

I can't speak. I'm reliving the moment the mud and limestone fell earlier: thudding down, blocking the light, the air, the way out. I'm fighting for breath, my chest heaving. My phone falls from my mouth, landing on its back and sending the torchlight straight up, into my eyes.

I shut them tight, frozen to the spot.

The rock fell before. Suppose it falls again?

There must be way more limestone pressing down on this passage than there was mud on top of the overhang. What if the roof caves in? What if rock fills the small space that we're in before we can crawl back out? What if we're buried alive?

'Ellie?' Harlan's voice is gentle. I vaguely notice, under my panic, that he's using my pet name again.

'I'm fine,' I insist, but my voice sounds tiny and fragile to my ears. 'I'm just worried about the rock falling in. Like ... like ... happened earlier.'

'It *won't*.' There's a firmness in Harlan's voice, a strength that reminds me of Dad's. 'We're too far inside the hill. The overhang was wide and thin. Fragile. It collapsed under the weight of the mud from the landslide. But these passageways are made by water eroding the limestone – they've been here for tens of thousands of years. They're not going to fall in on us today.'

'Okay.' I try to take in what he's saying, forcing my attention to the solid rock beneath my hands and knees. I breathe out, into the ground, remembering Dad's instructions. Silently I count, letting the full breath out until fresh air flows in.

'Ellie? You ready?' Harlan asks.

'Almost.' I open my eyes.

This tunnel is our only option. Wherever it leads has to be better than sitting in a cold cave waiting to die. I take and release another couple of deep breaths.

'I'm ready,' I say. 'I'm okay – the tunnel just freaked me out. It's so much smaller than the cave.'

There's a pause, then Harlan says, 'Technically it's not a tunnel. Tunnels are man-made, like the quarry. This is natural.'

'Right.' I grimace. 'Thanks for the science lesson.'

'Actually it's more geography, but whatever.' Harlan's voice is as ironic as my own. 'Always happy to help.'

I roll my eyes, but I'm grinning, in spite of myself. I pick up my phone and shove it into my mouth, spitting out the flecks of dirt on my lips. The torch lights up my path. I take another deep breath and start moving again, one hand and knee after the other. Behind me the soft thud of Harlan's hands and knees echo mine. He might have stopped wanting to be friends with me for no good reason, but I'm glad he's here.

Together, we shuffle through the tunnel. It feels like we go for miles. The air is somehow deadened here. Cold, but stuffy. The stone underneath us is hard and uneven. My knees and the heels of my hands are already sore. I reach down the legs of my trousers. The cotton fabric has torn at the knee, exposing my bare skin.

'D'you feel that?' Harlan asks.

I stop. 'What?' I press my palms against the walls of the narrow tunnel and turn my head, shining the torchlight around me. 'D'you think there'll be another cave-in?'

'No,' Harlan says. 'It's the air. I'm sure I just felt it get cooler, like we're getting closer to an exit.'

I frown, trying to work out if he's right.

'I dunno,' I say. 'It doesn't seem any different to me.'

Harlan says nothing. We carry on crawling along the narrow tunnel. Fresh fear grips me. Suppose we get stuck here? There's no way to turn around. We'd have to shuffle backwards just to get back to the cave.

I press my hands against the hard ground, trying to calm myself. We crawl on. My jaw is sore from gripping the phone between my teeth. After another minute or so, the tunnel widens again. I stop for a second, taking out my mobile to give my mouth a rest. I blow out my breath, relieved.

Behind me, Harlan pats the ground. *Thud, thud.* 'I think the air's getting colder again.' He sounds excited. 'I'm sure we're getting near a way out.'

'It could just be colder because we're getting deeper underground,' I mutter.

'There's no need to knock everything I'm saying.'

'I'm just being realistic,' I snap. 'It doesn't help me, you being all positive and raising my hopes when—'

'Well, it doesn't help *me*, you being all negative and dashing mine.'

'Tell you what, I'll shut up if you – oh.' I stare at the tunnel ahead. 'Oh, no.'

'What?' Harlan's voice fills with urgency. 'What's the matter? Is it getting narrower again?'

'No,' I say. 'Look.' I shove my phone back in my mouth and crawl another few metres. The tunnel opens out. There's even room to turn around. I sit to the side, then take my mobile into my hand and shine its light on the route ahead, glancing back at Harlan's shadowy face, dancing in the glow from his own mobile. A second later he's reached me.

'Oh,' says Harlan. 'I see.'

We stare, together, at the tunnel in front of us, at the place where it forks into two.

'How do we . . . ?' Harlan trails off, but I know what he's about to ask.

How do we know which of the two paths to take?

THIRTEEN

I wriggle closer to the openings, shining the light from my torch app into the darkness. There's nothing to choose between the two passageways. I sit back and glance at Harlan. 'What do we do?' I ask.

'I don't know.' He peers at his phone, his tanned skin pale in the glow of its screen.

'We've been in here ages. Do you think the others are back at camp yet? That they realize we're missing?'

I make a face. 'Mum and Dad'll be worried sick.'

'My mum will be too.' Harlan shudders. 'I'm down to twelve per cent battery,' he says. 'How about you?'

I glance at my own mobile. 'Twenty-five per cent,' I say, looking up.

Harlan meets my gaze. 'It won't be much fun when we run out of power.'

A shiver slithers down my spine. 'Then we need to get going again.' I point to the right-hand fork in the tunnel. 'Let's take that one. See where it goes.'

'Hang on. Why don't we each take one passage and see where it leads?' Harlan suggests.

'You mean, *separate*?' My stomach twists with anxiety. The last thing I want is to be crawling along these narrow tunnels on my own.

'Just for a minute,' Harlan urges. 'We could each take one passage and go down a little way into it, to a count of fifty, say, then come back and say where it leads. What it's like. If there's a way out.'

'How will we know?'

Harlan shrugs. 'Maybe we won't, but at least we'll have checked out both options.'

'Okay,' I agree, though privately I'm doubtful that either tunnel will tell us much. I'd still rather just plunge into one of them and crawl through it as fast as we can. 'But only to a count of fifty, yeah?'

'Sure.' Harlan points to the right-hand passage. 'You take that one. I'll do the one on the left.' He shoves his phone between his teeth. 'Let's go,' he says, the words muffled by the device.

We set off. I count under my breath – for the first ten counts I can still hear the echo of Harlan's padding in the neighbouring tunnel. Then that fades, and for ten more counts the only sound is my own shallow breathing. I'm suddenly aware of how completely alone I am, the whole hillside stacked on top of me. Panic rises inside me again. How can Harlan be so sure that the tons of limestone above us won't collapse into the passage? My mind races, trying to remember anything I was ever taught or had ever read about the science of rocks. I come up blank. I wish Harlan was with me.

I breathe out slowly, concentrating again on the damp limestone under my knees and hands. I'm cold and sore, but the ground is solid. I try to focus my breath through my body, into the stone beneath me. A long breath out, right to the end.

My racing heart slows.

Damn, I've lost count.

Where was I? At thirty? Forty? I start again at thirty-five, muttering under my breath: 'Thirty-six ... Thirty-seven ... Thirty-eight.'

When I get out of here ... *if* I get out of here ... I'm going to find out exactly what stops passageways like these from collapsing.

I've lost count *again*. Surely I must be at forty-five now? I'm just thinking that there's no way to tell whether I'm going towards an exit when, like magic, the light from my phone bumps and expands and I realize that the space around me is wider. Definitely wide enough to turn around in. I look up. It's higher too, no longer pressing down on my head. Excitement surges through me as I speed up, ignoring the bruising pain of my knees and hands. *Yes* – the whole tunnel is opening up!

I stand up, stretching out my arms, my jaw dropping as I shine my light around the cave I've just found. It's massive, the size of three houses. Maybe bigger. The ceiling is high above me, covered with hundreds of gleaming limestone spikes. They descend like icicles: all different sizes and lengths. They're beautiful. I grin, delight and relief coursing through my whole body.

'Ellie!' Harlan's desperate cry breaks the silence. *'Ellie!* Come back!'

FOURTEEN

'I'm coming!' I yell.

I'm so frantic to reach him that I barely notice the pain that shoots through my hands and knees as I hurry back to the fork in the tunnel. The musty smell of the damp limestone fills my nostrils. Harlan's phone light is a dim flicker in the distance at first, but quickly gets stronger. Harlan himself is cross-legged on the ground. As I approach, I notice the knees of his trousers, like mine, are ripped, revealing raw, red skin underneath.

'There you are,' he says, sounding relieved. 'You were so long that I—'

'I've found a massive cave!' I cry, crawling out of my tunnel. 'Somewhere we can stand up.'

'Well, I've found a way out!' Harlan's eyes shine with excitement.

'An actual exit?' I gasp.

'No,' he admits. 'But I felt fresh air. I think I did anyway.'

'But my passageway opens out into a cave. It's amazing, full of stone spikes hanging from the ceiling.' The words tumble out of me.

'They're called stalactites.' Harlan isn't smiling. 'And so what?'

'Surely the fact that it's so big means it's close to an exit, like the cave we were in before was close to the entrance.'

'That doesn't make any sense,' Harlan snaps. 'Just because it's big, doesn't mean it's close to anything. Did you feel a breeze at all? Because I did in *mine*.'

'But did your tunnel get bigger?' I demand.

'No – in fact it got smaller.' Harlan frowns. 'What's that got to do with it?'

I look down at the cold, hard ground. How can I explain to Harlan how terrified being in the low, cramped passage makes me? How anything is better than crawling along, panic swirling in my chest that the whole hill might collapse on top of me?

'We should go down *my* tunnel,' I insist, doggedly. 'Then we can stand up.'

'That's stupid.' Harlan shoots me a look of contempt. 'Fresh air means a way out.'

The silence hangs between us. I bite my lip. Harlan's right. Of course he is. I just don't want to accept it.

'But you said your tunnel got smaller.' My voice sounds strange to my ears. Stubborn and angry and broken.

'So *what?*' Harlan's voice rises. 'What is *wrong* with you? Man, I knew you were the most selfish person I'd ever met, but I didn't realize you were the most *stupid.*'

I stare at him, fury rising in me like acid. '*You're* the one being stupid,' I shout. 'Refusing to listen to me. Just like before, over Jake. *You're* stupid. And selfish.'

'*I'm* selfish?' he splutters. 'How do you—?'

'You won't listen to my side of things about Jake. And you were being *totally* selfish when you went into the woods and ended up at the bottom of the quarry—'

'I was trying to find *Boomer*!' Harlan explodes. 'And if—'

'If you'd kept him on a lead like you were supposed to by the trees, he wouldn't have got away,' I snap. 'You've lost him again now anyway. *And* thanks to you we're stuck in these horrible tunnels, which—'

'They're not *tunnels*. I already told you. Tunnels are *man-made*. These are naturally forming—'

'So *what*?' I suck in a huge, juddering breath and yell, 'You make out like you're such a victim, but the truth is you only think about yourself. And now we're going to *die* and it's *all your fault*!'

Harlan's eyes widen in the flickering light. I'm expecting him to yell back at me, but instead his voice drops very low. 'You shouldn't have told Jake how I felt,' he mutters.

'Why not?' I demand. 'You *liked* him.'

'Exactly, it was up to me to tell Jake I liked him. Not you. He told a bunch of people I was into him.' His voice cracks. 'It ... it was humiliating.'

I stare at him. 'Jake *told* people?'

'Yeah, and he made it quite clear he had no interest in me, which, if you'd given me the chance, I could have found out by myself, in my own time. In my own way.'

'Oh.' I hesitate, unsure what to say.

'So right now, I don't care what you do, *Ellen*,' Harlan says, stressing my name with total disdain. 'Go whichever way you like.'

And before I can speak a word, he plunges into the passageway on the left. Seconds later, he's disappeared from view.

FIFTEEN

I sit stock still, too shocked for a moment to speak or think. Has Harlan really abandoned me here? I glance at my phone. The torch app is sucking up the battery – it's down to eighteen per cent. Soon I'll be plunged into darkness.

Fear spirals through me. The last thing I want is to follow Harlan into an even narrower passage than this one, but, though I hate to admit it, he's right: fresh air means a way out. *Of course* it does.

I take a deep breath and dive after him. I crawl fast, the twists of anxiety in my chest tying themselves into tighter and tighter knots. Pain shoots through my hands and knees, but I can deal with that. What I can't take is the shadowy, spooky tunnel, the feeling that the walls are pressing in, the sense that I'm barely able to breathe.

Harlan's torch app is a tiny, flickering light in the distance. I hurry towards it, my breath coming in jagged, shallow gasps. Harlan shouldn't have left me behind. He's being totally unreasonable. How was I to know Jake would tell people Harlan liked him? It's not down to me that Harlan ended up feeling humiliated. I recall my words to him:

We're going to die and it's all your fault!

Okay, so it was mean of me to blame him for all of this, but Harlan's in the wrong too. Ahead of me, his light stops flickering, then looms larger as I draw closer. Harlan has stopped moving. He's bending around, peering back along the passageway.

Our eyes meet.

'You took your time,' he grunts.

I open my mouth, heart thudding. Part of me – a big part – wants to say sorry for my angry accusations a few minutes ago. But it's like Harlan's keeping some kind of invisible barrier up between us, and the words stay stuck in my throat.

'My phone's about to die,' Harlan says. 'I've only got –' As he speaks, the light from his phone goes out. 'Great,' he mutters.

'Here.' I hold out my own mobile. Its light wobbles in the gloomy tunnel. Another wave of fear washes over me. How much longer till my own battery dies?

'Don't you want this?' Harlan asks, taking the phone.

'You're the one in front,' I point out.

Harlan nods. 'Let's go,' he says. 'We're almost at the place where I felt the fresh air.'

'Good.' I breathe in and out slowly, trying to keep myself calm as we set off again. The dank, cold press of the limestone under my hands and knees gets more and more painful with every crawl. At least, now I'm back with Harlan, the tightness in my chest has eased a little.

I keep my eyes fixed on the ground ahead, on the soles of Harlan's shoes, watching as the light from the torch app bounces and sparks like a match up the sides of the walls. I try not to look at the walls, or think about how close they are. Above all, I avoid looking up. A rushing, buzzing feeling swarms my head, like an army of angry bees. Panic rises again, tightening my throat. The air here is so stuffy. Harlan must have been wrong about feeling a breeze, which surely means we're just going deeper and deeper into the hill?

I breathe in and out slowly, imagining Dad's gentle voice: *Calm down. Calm down, Ellie.*

We crawl on in silence. The tunnel narrows, like Harlan said. I try to keep my mind on my breathing.

In . . . out . . . in . . . out . . .

I still can't feel as much as a wisp of fresh air. The ground slopes upward, making the pressure on our knees even greater than before. I grit my teeth, trying to ignore the pain now shooting down my legs.

In . . . out . . . in . . . out . . .

Without warning, the light from my phone goes

SIXTEEN

A scream echoes around the tunnel.

It takes a second for me to realize it's me making the sound. Fear rises up into my throat, out of my mouth, the panic taking me over. Harlan has somehow turned around to face me. His hand is groping at my arm in the darkness, reaching for my hand, but I'm only vaguely aware of his touch ... his voice ...

'Ellie,' he's saying.

'AAAAAGGGGHHHH!' I shriek again.

'Ellie, *Ellie*.' Harlan is shaking me now. 'I know you're scared, but you're okay. We're okay. Everything's going to be all right.'

At last I hear his words and, even though I don't believe them, I hurl myself into his arms, sobbing now like my heart might break.

'We're going to die, the rock's going to collapse on top of us and we'll be buried alive and there's no light and ... and ...' I dissolve into tears, my face pressed against Harlan's shirt. The smell of dirt and sweat fills my nostrils. I squeeze my eyes tight shut. My breath is still coming in shaky gasps. I force out a long, slow exhalation. My heart is racing.

'We're not going to die,' Harlan says firmly. 'Can't you feel it? The breeze?'

I lift my head from his shoulder and open my eyes. The passage is pitch black, but I can feel the air now, chilling my cheek where my tears have left the skin damp.

I hug Harlan again. 'Yes!' I gasp. 'I feel it.'

'Come on.' Harlan draws away, but I tug him back.

'Wait a sec.' His angry, miserable words from before echo in my head:

It was up to me to tell Jake I liked him. Not you . . .

He told a bunch of people I was into him. It . . . it was humiliating.

How would I feel if I'd been in Harlan's position? Probably I'd feel humiliated too. And angry with whoever had blabbed to the boy I liked. It hits me, as hard and cold as ice water, that I shouldn't have interfered.

'What is it?' Harlan asks.

I let out a shaky breath. 'You were right about Jake. I shouldn't have told him how you felt. It was . . . thoughtless. I promise I never dreamed he'd be mean about it.'

Harlan sighs in the darkness. 'I don't think Jake meant to be mean – he was just being thoughtless too, not thinking how I'd feel.'

'Yeah,' I say, 'but Jake doesn't know you. You're my . . . my best friend. You've every right to be angry. I'm sorry.'

'Thanks,' Harlan says gruffly. 'If I'm honest, it's easier to be angry with you than think about Jake humiliating me.' I can hear the pain in his voice. 'But I know you didn't mean to . . . to upset me.'

He draws away again and, this time, I let him go. He clears his throat. 'Let's find that exit.'

He squeezes himself around to face forward and we crawl on, faster now in spite of the hard, damp limestone shooting daggers of pain into our knees.

'D'you think it's wetter because of the rain from outside?' I ask.

'It could just be the limestone,' Harlan says. 'It's porous. That's how these passages form, remember? Rain eroding the rock. Oh, look!'

I crane forward, peering past him. A soft glow radiates in the distance. 'Daylight!' I cry.

'We've done it!' Harlan's relieved voice echoes around the passageway.

We hurry towards the light. Soon it morphs into actual blue sky. My heart lifts, the pain in my knees miraculously disappearing in the excitement. And, suddenly, we're crawling outside. I breathe in the sweet smell of the fresh air as we emerge on to a narrow ledge, barely the size of a bus seat. The stark limestone quarry surrounds us, damp from the recent rain. Dislodged pebbles skitter away as

I unfurl my sore legs, squinting against the glare of the natural light.

'Oh, man!' Harlan presses back against the rock, his face draining of colour. 'This does *not* feel safe.'

I look down and my head spins. We're at least thirty metres above the ground – too far to jump. Across the quarry, I spot the remains of the overhang above the cave where Boomer got stuck. Huge chunks of mud and massive slabs of limestone are piled high on the ground in front of the entrance. I shiver at the sight.

'That's where we came in,' I say, pointing. 'We must have crawled all this way uphill.'

'But how much further is there to go?' Harlan asks

A cold feeling of dread creeps over me. If we're only thirty metres or so above ground, how far above us does the quarry rise?

I lift my head. *Oh, no.* The rock face above looms high over our heads. It must be at least sixty more metres to the top. Worse, it's as smooth as ice and far steeper than the patch that I tumbled down earlier. Surely impossible to climb. The reality of our situation hits me like a punch.

We're as trapped as we were before.

SEVENTEEN

Harlan squints out across the quarry, his back still firmly pressed against the rock face. 'I think it's going to rain again. Look!'

I follow his gaze. The sun's orange glow is half hidden behind a steel-grey cloud. More clouds are gathering, scudding across the sky. My eyes automatically flicker to my phone, which of course is now just a lump of plastic and a blank screen.

Harlan shivers. 'I hope Boomer's all right.'

'I'm sure he is.' I squeeze Harlan's hand. 'He got out of the cave before the rocks piled up, remember? And dogs are great at finding their way back home.'

Harlan nods, though he doesn't look entirely convinced. The wind whips up, a strong gust battering our bodies. The blue above us is disappearing, leaving the sky dark and threatening. A rumble of thunder sounds in the distance. I strain to see the side of the rock face from which our ledge sticks out. The climb to the top might look impossible, but if we don't attempt it, we'll be stuck here all night. The quarry is deserted. We have no way of calling anyone. No warm clothes or light. No food. Not even any water. As I think this, I realize how thirsty I am.

Harlan glances back into the long, cramped passageway. There are shadows under his eyes from the effort of our crawl. His hands shake as he rubs anxiously at his forehead. 'Do you think we should go back? See if there's another way out?' he asks. 'That other passageway ... ?'

I meet his gaze. I can see the fear in his eyes and the last thing I want is to make him feel worse. But there's no point lying to him. 'No,' I say firmly. 'We have to climb.' I scan the smooth, grey quarry-side above us again. Looking more closely, I spot small ridges and dips in the surface. 'We can use those as handholds,' I say, pointing. 'Come on, we can do this.'

Harlan shakes his head. 'I can't,' he says. 'I'm . . . It's . . .' He looks down, shame flushing his face. 'I'm too scared.'

The old me would have brushed this aside, told him there was nothing to worry about. But imagine if Harlan feels as terrified as I did when the light went out in the passageway? Maybe I should do what he did then?

I reach across and pat his arm. It's as grazed and bruised as mine. 'It *is* a bit scary,' I say. 'But you can do it.'

Harlan shakes his head again. 'I'm not sporty and brave like you. I didn't say earlier, but I only fell down the quarry in the first place because I freaked when I saw how steep it was. I'm . . . I'm a coward.' His voice cracks.

I snort. 'Then we both are,' I say. 'Remember how I acted in the cave?'

Harlan shrugs. 'That was a panic attack. You couldn't help it.'

'Whatever. You were amazing back then.' I pause. 'I wouldn't have made it out here without you.'

Harlan twists away, clearly embarrassed. 'Maybe you should go on ahead, on your own,' he mutters. 'Get help for me?'

'No. No way.' I shake my head for emphasis. 'I'm not leaving you. And I'm *certain* we can do this.'

Harlan looks up. 'Seriously?'

'Seriously,' I say. 'You're the bravest person I know.'

'Okay,' Harlan says. 'I'll do it, but only if you stop being so sappy.'

I stare at his grubby face. 'You know … I'm starting to wish I'd left you in that cave.'

Harlan laughs. 'I guess we're stuck with each other now.'

'Nice,' I say, grinning. 'Thanks.'

'Come on, then.' Harlan stands up, clinging to the rock behind him. 'Where do we start?'

'That way looks like there's more footholds.' I point to the left. Harlan nods. I rub my hands on my trousers. They are slippery with sweat and dirt and I need them to be able to grip the rocks as tightly as possible. The cloth over my knees has completely worn away. I catch sight of the grubby, bruised skin underneath, pain throbbing along my sore, cramped legs. Harlan must be feeling the same. I pray that the two of us will have the strength for this climb.

I reach out and grip a jutting piece of rock just above my head, then look for a foothold. *There.*

'Watch what I do,' I call to Harlan. 'Put your hands and feet where I put mine.'

He gulps. I give him an encouraging smile, then push off from the ledge. The wind whistles past as I cling to the rock face. I'd been worried I would slip off the stone, but my biggest problem is the pain from where the rock digs into my bruised, scratched palms. Swallowing down the discomfort, I glance across at Harlan.

'Take it one step at a time!' I shout over the wind. 'You can totally do this!'

He nods, his eyes wide with fear.

I take a deep breath and start climbing.

EIGHTEEN

I climb slowly, glancing back at Harlan after every move.

He's hesitant at first. But after a minute or so he speeds up, moving more confidently. I focus on the rock face above me, scanning for places where we can put our hands and feet. It's hot work, despite the cold wind, and I'm sweating, trying to ignore the pain that pulses from my hands up through my arms as I grip hard, reaching out my leg to find the next foothold.

'One step at a time, remember!' I yell, though the wind is stronger now and I'm not sure Harlan hears me.

Rain patters on to my head and back. Light at first, but then stronger, harder. I focus my gaze on the next stretch of rock. Harlan keeps pace with me, following my route up the rock face.

I glance up. The top of the quarry, which had looked so far away just a few minutes ago, is now in sight, just a body's length away.

'Hey!' I shout, blinking away the rain.

Harlan looks up.

I indicate the summit with my eyes. 'We're nearly there.'

Harlan nods. He grabs a piece of sticking-out rock above his head, then hauls himself up. I concentrate on the next handhold. My breath comes in rapid, shallow gasps as I step carefully, one small move at a time.

The limestone is cold and wet against my body. Properly slippery. And my arms and legs are tired. Just one more heave. *There.* I reach the top of the quarry and clamber over. I lie, catching my breath for a second, then peer down. The ground is a dizzying distance away. The rain stops at last.

Harlan is still climbing, about a metre below me. He gazes up and meets my eyes. His whole face is wreathed in panic.

'I can't see a handhold!' He gasps. 'It's too slippy. I'm losing my grip.'

My heart races as I desperately scan the rock face between us.

'There!' I point to a stony hook. 'Get your hand on that and I'll help you up.'

With a huge groan, Harlan heaves himself up. His hand scrabbles wildly for purchase. For a single, terrifying second I freeze. He can't fall. Not Harlan.

My best and oldest friend.

'Grab the rock!' I yell.

Harlan's left hand clamps on the jutting-out piece of stone. He hauls himself up, his right hand finding the top of the quarry.

'You've done it!' I cry. I lean over to help him. My hand grips his arm, tugging him towards me. 'Come on!'

Harlan lets out another huge groan of effort. He

gets one leg over the ledge and I'm clawing under his arm now, trying to help him bring up the other leg. And then time slows down as Harlan shifts his weight and my hand slips on the wet rock and somehow I lose my balance.

And fall.

NINETEEN

Falling in slow motion, my hand slides down Harlan's arm.

'AAAGGH!' I scream, clutching at his fingers.

He grips me hard. I dangle off the rock face, my legs wheeling, my arm feeling like it's being wrenched out of its socket.

'Ellie!' Harlan shouts. 'Do something!'

Something in his panicking voice makes me stop moving. I stare up, my eyes blinking back the rain. I find the handhold I used before and, still gripping his fingers with one hand, I reach out with my other and grab it. I press my feet against the rock face, feeling for footholds. *There.* I haul myself higher, Harlan dragging me up by my hand. I find the quarry top and slam my palm down. Harlan reaches down, grabs me under both armpits.

He pulls as I heave myself on to the broad ledge.

I lie, panting, on the ground. 'We *did it*!' I gasp.

Harlan wriggles away from the edge. 'I am *never* climbing *anything* again,' he says.

I sit up shakily and then somehow we're in each other's arms, laughing and crying with joy and relief.

It's the fiercest, truest, best hug of my life.

'Thank you,' we both say at the same time then, slowly, draw apart.

Suddenly I'm so tired I can barely move.

High above the quarry, the sun emerges fully from behind its cloud. The sky is filling with pink and orange swirls, all the dark clouds skittering away.

'Come on,' I say. 'Let's get back to camp.'

Harlan is gazing around, trying to get his bearings.

'Where are we?' I ask.

Harlan points towards a large house, just visible in the distance, two fields over.

'Is that the farmhouse?' he asks.

I nod excitedly. 'Yes – so our camp must be over there.' I point to the right of the building.

We start walking. Every bit of me aches. My clothes, face and hands are covered in dust and dirt, and my knees and hands are bruised and sore. I glance at Harlan. His face is twisted with anxiety.

'Are you worrying about Boomer?' I ask.

He nods. 'Let's call him.'

'Boomer! Boomer!' we yell.

Nothing. We cross the fields in sombre silence, the sky now clear above our heads. Over the stile and across the next field. We can see the farmhouse properly now. And the smoke flying up from the fire in the middle of our camp.

Suddenly, tearing across the grass like a bullet, Boomer bounds towards us.

'Yes!' we cry out together, as the dog leaps

up – first at Harlan, then me – his tail wagging furiously.

Harlan drops to the earth, burying his face in Boomer's fur. I fill up with happiness.

We made it. We survived. All of us.

'Ellen! Harlan!' Dad's anxious cry drifts towards us.

We look at each other and break into a run, Boomer bounding at our side. A minute later, we're past the farmhouse and racing into our field.

Dad is right there.

'Ellie!' he calls out.

'Dad!' I shout.

The fear on his face dissolves into relief as he races towards me.

'Lauren!' he calls to Mum. 'She's here!'

I run harder, bursting into tears as Dad reaches me, pulling me into a huge embrace.

We're both crying now. And then suddenly everyone is here, and Mum takes me in her arms too. Charlie grabs my leg and won't let go while Auntie Mo gabbles away, saying how they got back to the camp an hour ago, to find Boomer barking non-stop. And suddenly everyone's talking at once: how worried they've been, how they were going to call the police if we weren't back soon, asking where we were and what happened.

I glance across at Harlan. He's trying to wriggle out of his mum's arms, but Auntie Juniper is holding him fast. At last our parents release us.

'What happened?' Dad asks.

'Did you get lost?' Mum asks.

'Are you hurt?' Auntie Juniper asks.

'How come you're covered in dirt?' Auntie Mo adds.

I meet Harlan's gaze and smile.

'We're okay,' I say, 'thanks to Harlan. He saved Boomer.' I think about my panicky fear in the passage. 'And me.'

'Actually Ellie saved *me*,' Harlan says. 'We had to climb up the quarry. It was *horrible*.'

I glance at Dad. He's shaking his head.

'I know we broke the rules,' I say quickly. 'But there was a landslide. If Harlan hadn't gone after Boomer, he'd have been trapped in a cave and died.'

Dad nods. Then sighs. 'I'm just glad you're all okay.'

I reach out and punch Harlan, very lightly, on the arm. 'We're more than okay,' I say.

'Yeah.' Harlan smiles. And I see in his eyes that the boy who was missing, my best friend in the whole world, is back.

Sophie McKenzie

TRUTH
OR
DARE

Million copy selling author of **GIRL, MISSING**

WHEN LIES ARE EVERYWHERE, HOW FAR WILL YOU GO FOR THE TRUTH?

Read on for an
EXCLUSIVE EXTRACT
from Sophie McKenzie's explosive
new thriller - *Truth or Dare*

APRIL 2022

SIMON &
SCHUSTER

The train slows to a stop somewhere between stations. On one side a row of trees grows close to the track, sunlight dancing through their green, swaying branches. On the other an expanse of empty fields is spread out as far as the eye can see.

This is the countryside. Where literally nothing is happening. And I'm going to be stuck here for the rest of the summer.

It's my worst nightmare.

Leo fidgets on the seat opposite me. His pale, earnest face is turned, as usual, towards his phone. Leo is nine, five years younger than me, but he's not like most kids his age. He knows some things in depth, like stuff about engines and volcanoes and electricity, that your average uni professor wouldn't have a clue about. Then there's other things, like talking to people in real life, where he still acts like a tiny kid.

Mum ruffles his hair, then tucks her own behind her ears. She hasn't taken her eyes off her laptop this whole journey except to dole out sandwiches for lunch an hour or so ago.

'How many more stops?' I ask, as the train starts moving again.

Mum looks up from her work, frowning. She never stops working these days. 'What was the last station?' she asks.

'Polborne,' says Leo. I have no idea how he knows. I swear he didn't look up once when we were in the station.

Mum's eyes spark with alarm. 'Next stop then,' she says, grabbing the papers which litter our table and shoving them in her tote. 'Maya, fetch our bags down please.'

I heave a sigh and get up.

'Is that when you're leaving us, Mum?' Leo asks, a note of anxiety creeping into his voice.

'That's where Gran is picking you up,' Mum counters, brightly.

I glance at Leo. His solemn eyes meet mine and I force a smile. I want to reasure him, but I'm as upset as he is at the prospect of spending the next six weeks with our grandparents. Right now, back in London, my friends will be in the park – chatting and playing music and talking about the parties planned for this weekend.

And I'm missing all of it.

'Maya, *please*. The bags.'

'Okay, Mum, I'm *doing* it.'

The train slows, the brakes screeching loudly as it pulls into a tiny station. Leo puts his hands over his ears; he hates loud noises. I fetch Leo's bag and my suitcase down from the overhead rack, then lug them along the aisle. Nobody else is getting off.

'Come on Leo,' Mum urges, her voice rising behind me. 'The noise has stopped now. Make sure you've got your phone with you and don't forget your rucksack.'

I press the door release button and step onto the platform. After the chill of the air-conditioned carriage, the sun is fierce on my face. My suitcase is heavy, the handle digging into my palm. I set it down on the platform, as Mum and Leo emerge from the train. Leo squints up and down. 'I don't see Gran,' he says.

'She'll be out in the car park.' Mum dives into her cluttered shoulder bag and pulls out her phone. She checks the screen, an anxious frown on her face. 'Right, I've got ten minutes before my train back to Plymouth. I mustn't miss my connection.'

I follow the two of them along the platform, feeling sullen. The sun beats down on my face and back. I'm too hot in my long-sleeved, crop top and black joggers. A stray thread has frayed and dangles off the sleeve and I tug it off. I get an allowance from Mum which I spend mostly online at Bonropa. The clothes there are cheap – and do tend to fray or twist out of shape – but they look great for the first few wears. Just because I'm going to be away from civilisation for a month, doesn't mean I have to let standards slip.

In the carpark, a woman with a silvery bob steps out from behind the shiniest, sleekest car.

'There she is,' Mum says, sounding relieved.

Gran strides towards us. She's dressed in crisp navy trousers, kitten heels, and a silk grey blouse. She might be old but she knows how to style herself. Unlike Mum, with her shapeless dress and damp strands of hair plastered over her forehead, Gran looks smart and elegant. Even her nails are perfect: painted a pearly pink that picks out the exact shade of her lipstick.

'Hi.' Mum sounds wary as Gran approaches.

'Hello, love.' Gran leans in to peck Mum on the cheek, then pats Leo on the shoulder and nods at me. The sun glints off the delicate gold chain around her neck. 'It's wonderful to see you all.' I'd forgotten how brisk she is – every movement precise. 'Good journey?'

'Fine,' Mum says, shifting her bulging bag higher

up her shoulder. 'But I have to go I'm afraid. Make my connection to Bristol. Evening drinks on the first night of a conference is the biggest networking opportunity of the weekend.'

Gran looks Mum up and down. A disapproving gleam creeps into her eyes. 'Well, I hope you're going to put on something a little more formal before you start mingling,' she says, briskly. 'And, darling, I'm only saying this because I love you, but you really need to do something about that hair.'

My jaw drops. There's an awkward silence.

'Right,' mutters Mum. She looks like she wants to say more, but stops herself. Instead, she turns to Leo and pulls him into her arms. Leo submits even though he's never been a big fan of hugging. 'Be a good boy for Gran and Grandad.' Mum turns to me.' Don't spend *all* your time on your phone, Maya. Get outside ... where it's safe obviously.'

'Bye, Mum,' I say, though what I'm thinking is that Leo spends way more time on his phone than I do.

Leo' bottom lip trembles.

'Well, no point in long, drawn-out goodbyes,' Gran says.

Mum gives Leo a final kiss, wraps her arms around me for a short, fierce hug, then turns quickly away. One of the laces on her trainer trails in the dust as she disappears back onto the platform. Leo stares after her, clearly trying hard not to cry.

I feel numb, as the reality of this nightmare summer in the middle of nowhere settles like a stone in my guts.

'Come along,' Gran says briskly. 'I need to pop into work.'

Leo and I hurry after her. 'Work?' I ask. 'Aren't we going to your house?'

'As soon as I've checked one thing at the factory.' Gran opens the boot of her shiny car and we dump our luggage inside. 'Leo, you sit in the back. Seatbelt on, please. Maya, up front with me.' There's a way she has of speaking which doesn't allow for disagreement. Leo obediently scrambles into the back seat. I hesitate, my hand on the car door.

'In you get, Maya,' Gran urges, sliding elegantly into the driver's seat. 'I'm sure you'll be pleased to hear that we've introduced lots of new green measures at the factory since you were last here.'

'Oh.' I shrug. I barely remember anything about the factory, but the last thing I want is to encourage Gran to talk about it.

'Yes, Peyton Soaps is moving with the times and much more environmentally friendly than it used to be,' Gran says as we head out of the car park. 'I've changed lots of our production methods and made sure *all* our wastewater is properly treated and *all* our rubbish is taken to certified recycling facilities.' She pats the steering wheel.

'Great,' I mutter, rolling my eyes.

'What's wastewater?' Leo asks. 'And what does 'treating' it mean?'

'Ah, well,' Gran says, 'there's an interesting process known as flocculation, which ...' I stop listening and stare out of the window, feeling more and more depressed. The glass is tinted, which makes the hedges and fields we're speeding past look dull and grey. Ten minutes pass and we don't see so much as another car, let alone a building. How on earth am I going to survive the next six weeks? Gran starts talking about the history of Peyton Soaps, telling Leo the story I already know: how it was set up as a family business sixty years ago by Gran's father and is now one of the biggest employers in the area.

We take the turning for Penwillick and the road narrows as we approach a low bridge.

'We're almost at the factory,' Gran says.

I gaze out, over a glistening stream. It stretches away from the road, towards an explanse of woodland a few metres away. A group of five or six people are examining one of the trees. Most of them are in shadow, but one boy about my age and dressed in shorts and a t-shirt, is standing in a pool of light, his hair glinting like a halo. A little girl in a pinafore dress runs over, jumping up and down in front of him.

As we draw closer, the boy looks up. He scowls at the car.

Even though I know he can't see me through the tinted window, I shrink back. Why is he glowering at us like that?

Gran gives a tut as we drive away, over the bridge.

'I see the eco-nutters are out in force today,' she says, a particularly sharp edge to her voice.

'Eco-nutters?' I ask.

'Bunch of hippies who live in Penwillick Wood,' Gran explains. 'Despite my best efforts they got council permission to build a small community in the wood a few years ago.

'Why did you object?' I ask, feeling confused. Didn't Gran just say how environmentally friendly her company was?

Gran shoots a frown at me. 'I don't want a group of smug, grubby activists camped in my neighbourhood,' she says. 'I lodged a fresh appeal against their community a few months ago, but I don't hold out much hope. These days anything remotely green-sounding gets a pass, no matter how much it costs everyone else.'

'I thought Peyton Soaps was all about being green?' I ask.

'That's completely different,' Gran says with a sniff. 'Those eco-nutters are extremists. Prepared to go to any lengths to get what they want.'

I turn and look out through the back window of the car. The boy is still glaring at us.

A shiver snakes down my spine.

Sophie
McKenzie

Discover the bestselling **MISSING SERIES** from the queen of teen thrillers.

'Sophie's thrillers are in a league of their own – nobody does it better'
Phil Earle, author of *When the Sky Falls*

SIMON &
SCHUSTER

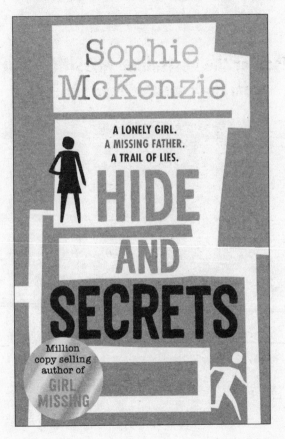

SIMON & SCHUSTER

ABOUT THE AUTHOR

Sophie McKenzie is the multi award-winning original queen of teen thrillers, whose debut, *Girl, Missing*, first published in 2006, remains a YA bestseller. She has followed its success with two further books in the Missing series: *Sister, Missing* and *Missing Me*, as well as many other teen thriller and romance novels, including *Hide and Secrets* and The Medusa Project series. *Boy, Missing*, set in the world of the Missing series is a 2022 World Book Day selection and her next novel, *Truth or Dare*, will be published in April 2022. Sophie's books have sold more than a million copies in the UK alone and are translated and sold all over the world. She lives in North London.

www.sophiemckenziebooks.com
Twitter: @sophiemckenzie_

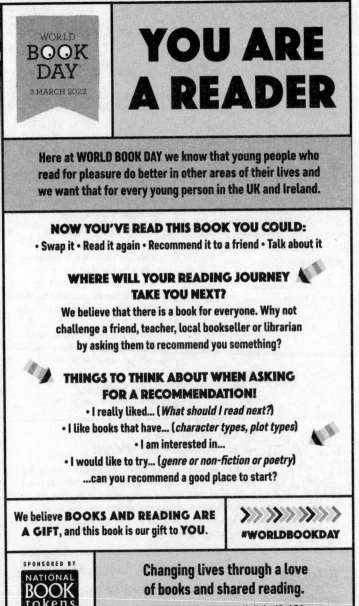

WORLD
BOOK
DAY
3 MARCH 2022

WHERE CAN YOU FIND YOUR NEXT READ? YOU CAN...

1 TAKE A TRIP TO YOUR LOCAL BOOKSHOP

Booksellers like nothing more than the challenge of finding the perfect book for someone. Don't worry if what you want isn't on the shelf, most are happy to order specific things in.

Find your local bookshop:
booksaremybag.com

2 JOIN YOUR LOCAL LIBRARY

Libraries are a great way to take a risk on a book for free. Most library services have an online catalogue so you can browse at home and even order books to be delivered to your local branch.

You can also access magazines, ebooks and audiobooks online at home or on the go, with your library membership.

Find your local library:
gov.uk/local-library-services/

3 CHECK OUT THE WORLD BOOK DAY WEBSITE

There are so many ways to find your next favourite book. Talk to your friends and find out what they're loving, or even check out social media like Tiktok and Instagram to find the latest top recommendations. You can visit worldbookday.com where we have brilliant reads for you to discover and videos of some of our top authors to enjoy.

SPONSORED BY

NATIONAL
BOOK
tokens

Changing lives through a love of books and shared reading.

World Book Day® is a charity sponsored by National Book Tokens